THE AMAZING ADVENTURES OF THE

DC SUPER-PETS!™

Magical Mischief

by **Steve Korté**

illustrated by **Mike Kunkel**

PICTURE WINDOW BOOKS
a capstone imprint

Published by Picture Window Books, an imprint of Capstone
1710 Roe Crest Drive
North Mankato, Minnesota 56003
capstonepub.com

Cataloging-in-Publication Data is available at the Library of Congress website.
ISBN: 9781484672105 (hardcover)
ISBN: 9781484672068 (paperback)
ISBN: 9781484672075 (ebook PDF)

Summary: Krypto is Superman's best friend. But when the
evil Mxy unleashes his magical mischief, the canine crime fighter
becomes the Man of Steel's worst enemy.

Designed by Elyse White

Printed and bound in the USA. PO# 5195

TABLE OF CONTENTS

CHAPTER 1
Trouble in Space 7

CHAPTER 2
Growing Pains 15

CHAPTER 3
Canine Conversation 23

He is Superman's loyal friend.
He came from the planet Krypton.
He has many of the same super-
powers as the Man of Steel.
These are . . .

THE AMAZING
ADVENTURES OF
Krypto the
Super-Dog!

Trouble in Space

Krypto the Super-Dog loves playing in space. He slams his super-strong head against an asteroid.

BLAM!

"Hey! What's the big idea?" yells an angry little man who was taking a nap on that asteroid.

The angry man is Mr. Mxyzptlk. He is a mischief-making imp from another world. He uses magic to cause trouble.

The only way to get rid of Mr. Mxyzptlk is to trick him into speaking his name backward.

"I'll teach that horrible hound to watch where's he flying!" says Mr. Mxyzptlk.

When they both arrive on Earth,

Mr. Mxyzptlk uses his mind to cast

a spell on Krypto.

He forces Krypto to fly to the *Daily*

Planet newspaper office. A reporter

named Clark Kent is working there.

Clark Kent is secretly the super hero Superman. Mr. Mxyzptlk hopes that Krypto's arrival at the *Daily Planet* will expose Superman's identity.

"What is Krypto doing here?" wonders Clark. *"I need to create a distraction."*

Clark focuses his eyes on a fire alarm. He uses his heat-vision to send a powerful ray of heat from his eyes toward the fire alarm.

The fire alarm rings. All of the employees rush out of the building.

"That was a close one, Krypto," says
Clark. "We need to get you out of here."

Clark quickly changes into his
Superman uniform. He flies to the roof
of the *Daily Planet* building. Krypto
follows him.

CHAPTER 2

Growing Pains

Then the evil Mr. Mxyzptlk has a new idea.

"I think I'll super-size this pesky pooch," says Mr. Mxyzptlk.

He magically makes Krypto grow and grow and grow. Soon Krypto is bigger than the metal globe on top of the *Daily Planet* building!

"Go fetch that big globe, you mangy

mutt!" Mr. Mxyzptlk says.

Krypto grabs the giant globe. He pulls

it from the building. Then he tosses it

over the side of the roof.

Superman zooms through the air to catch the globe before it can hurt anyone.

Just then, an airplane flies above the building.

"Time for a trip," says Mr. Mxyzptlk.

He magically orders Krypto to chase the plane.

Krypto flies away with Superman in pursuit. Krypto lands on top of an airplane, causing the plane to shake violently in the sky.

The Man of Steel uses his super-strength to pull Krypto off the plane.

"What's gotten into you, Krypto?" Superman asks.

"Now it's time for Superman to take a trip!" says Mr. Mxyzptlk.

The imp orders Krypto to grab Superman's cape. Krypto holds the cape and starts swinging the Man of Steel around. Faster and faster he spins.

Finally, Krypto lets go of the cape, sending Superman soaring into space.

Canine Conversation

Krypto lands on the ground, feeling confused. He can't understand why he is doing all these bad things.

"You deserve a reward for your bad behavior," Mr. Mxyzptlk says. "I am going to give you the power of speech!"

"Thank you," says Krypto. "I would like to start using a new name. I want a name that has nothing to do with Superman."

"Wonderful idea!" says Mr. Mxyzptlk.

"What name would you like?"

"Kltpzyxm," the Super-Dog replies.

Mr. Mxyzptlk says, "That's a strange name. Are you sure you want to be called Kltpzyxm—"

A look of horror fills Mr. Mxyzptlk's face. He has been tricked into speaking his name backward!

Mr. Mxyzptlk disappears in a cloud of smoke.

Superman returns just in time to see the magical imp vanish. With Mr. Mxyzptlk gone, Krypto shrinks down to his regular size.

"I'm sorry you don't have the power to talk anymore," says Superman. "But I'm glad you're back to normal."

The Super-Dog happily wags his tail and responds with the only word he can now speak.

"WOOF!"

AUTHOR!

Steve Korté is the author of many books for children and young adults. He worked at DC Comics for many years, editing more than 600 books about Superman, Batman, Wonder Woman, and the other heroes and villains in the DC Universe. He lives in New York City with his husband, Bill, and their super-cat, Duke.

ILLUSTRATOR!

Mike Kunkel wanted to be a cartoonist ever since he was a little kid. He has worked on numerous projects in animation and books, including many years spent drawing cartoon stories about creatures and super heroes such as the Smurfs and Shazam! He has won the Annie Award for Best Character Design in an Animated Television Production and is the creator of the two-time Eisner Award-winning comic book series *Herobear and the Kid*. Mike lives in southern California, and he spends most of his extra time drawing cartoons filled with puns, trying to learn new magic tricks, and playing games with his family.

"Word Power"

expose (ek-SPOHZ)—to reveal or unmask

imp (IMP)—a small creature that plays harmful tricks

mischief (MIS-chif)—action that causes trouble

Mxyzptlk (mix-eez-PIT-uhl-ik)—a creature from another dimension who likes to play tricks on others

pursuit (per-SOOT)—the act of following something in order to overtake it

spell (SPEL)—a word or words that are supposed to have magical powers

vanish (VAN-ish)—to disappear suddenly

WRITING PROMPTS

1. Superman and Krypto are best friends. Write about one of your best friends.

2. Make a list of your name and four of your friends. Now write everyone's names backward and try to pronounce them.

3. Mr. Mxyzptlk calls Krypto lots of names, including pesky pooch and horrible hound. Write a paragraph about Krypto using your own adjectives to describe him.

DISCUSSION QUESTIONS

1. Why do you think Mr. Mxyzptlk got mad so quickly when Krypto ran into the asteroid? Do you think his reaction was necessary?

2. What would you have done to distract the people in the newsroom when Krypto showed up?

3. Mr. Mxyzptlk gives Krypto the power of speech for his bad behavior. What other power could he have given Krypto?

THE AMAZING ADVENTURES OF THE DC SUPER-PETS!

Collect them all!